An Immortal Sorceress
NOVELLA

Fury of the Sorceress

KRISTA WALSH

Raven's Quill Press

Ottawa, ON

Raven's Quill Press

www.kristawalshauthor.com

Cover Design: Deranged Doctor Design/2023

Fury of the Sorceress / WALSH -- 1st ed.
Paperback ISBN: 978-1-7380240-1-8

To you

For joining me on this brand-new adventure

1

Katerina

VAMPIRES." I GROANED and bowed my head against the side of my phone before bringing it back to my ear. "I don't do vampires."

"To be fair, you've never given us a chance," Adrian said with an exaggerated air that earned him a smile.

"Fine, but unless you wow me, I'm not changing my mind."

I sat back in one of the Muskoka chairs on my bedroom patio and sipped my coffee. The sun had yet to rise, but I hadn't slept well, chased by dreams of blood magic and deadly rituals, silver eyes and soft words. It was a nice change of pace from the nightmares that had haunted me for the first few centuries of my immortality, but they made sleep a lukewarm wish.

The pre-dawn darkness created shadows that pressed the

trees closer to the house and hid Lake Huron from view. Only the rustle of the cold Canadian March wind through the bare branches and the lap of water against the icy shore connected me to the world beyond.

Elsewhere in the house, my housekeeper, Maera Byrne, and her eighteen-year-old son, Rhys, were huddled warm and snug in their beds. I didn't envy them. The silence of a world not yet awake made this my favourite time of day. Usually.

"There are vampire hunters to take care of nests that step out of line," I said as I channelled magic into my palms to warm my mug. "I've sworn off messing with you bitey bastards, you know that."

"A decision I've respected for a good many centuries, as you well know, but this case is different. I guarantee wowing you won't be an issue."

"Have at it."

"The nest governs the better part of an entire city."

Coffee lodged in my throat and dribbled down my lip. Grateful my old friend wasn't present to see the mess, I used the back of my bare hand to clear the stray drips away and cleared my throat. "Excuse me?"

"I thought that might get your attention."

I hated when Adrian got smug. After spending eight hundred years with him, I could safely say it was his least attractive trait.

"Explain."

"Have you ever been to Orillia?" he asked.

I scanned my memory until I caught a flash of a small Ontario city. "I've driven through it. Can't say I've ever stopped there. It's only a few hours away from you, isn't it?"

"It is, and for the past ten years, the vampire queen and I have lived with an easy understanding. She's ancient, one of the few vampires I know older than me, so she comes by for a drink now and again to pick my brain on immortality."

I sank back in my chair, took one more sip of coffee before setting it on the table, and pulled my feet onto the edge of the seat. "Interest levels dropping. Abort. Abort."

"She's gone missing. Her nest is concerned and growing restless, and their human thralls are behaving... strangely."

That pulled my attention out of the red. "And the whole 'nest governs a city' thing?"

"A critical piece of information if we don't solve this quickly. If the nest suspects the humans of Orillia had anything to do with their queen's disappearance and decides to do something about it, we might have a wide-scale massacre on our hands. For now, the queen's right hand has kept the others in check and convinced them to bring the matter to my attention."

"Expecting you to do what?"

Adrian had long since retired from the world, happy to sit in his library with a glass of vintage blood, a book on his lap, and his human thrall, James Barrett, standing alert and aloof behind him. For centuries, Adrian and I had worked together, dealing with magical threats, but he hadn't taken an active role in the hunt since saving Barrett's life a decade ago—and even that had been an exception.

"She expected me to reach out to you, Katerina." The *obviously* went unsaid but oozed through his tone.

My stomach dropped. "Of course."

"Despite your lack of engagement over the past few decades, your reputation stems from centuries of legend. You are Katerina of Palonia, sorceress, master of fire and lightning, queen of ice, guardian of the balance between magical and mundane, destroyer of evil."

"And?"

"And you live a few hours from Orillia. The queen's second turns to you because she believes you can help resolve their issue without having the business hub of Muskoka outed as one of the vampire capitals of the province."

I groaned, dropping my forehead to my knees. "No pressure."

"Not at all. I believe you can do it as well. Especially as I'll be there to help you."

That made me sit up. "You? Mr. I'm Never Working Up A Sweat Again?"

He scoffed. "I don't sweat."

"Metaphorically, of course. You smell of fresh-frosted

mornings and black roses."

"Are you flattering me to get out of my request or is it a veiled acceptance?"

"Can't it be both?" I asked.

"I'll drive to Orillia with James first thing tonight. If you're able to meet us there, I would appreciate it. Trillium—the queen's second—has a room for us in the nest."

My head swam. I didn't get along with most vampires at the best of times, so the idea of staying in their house was the least appealing part of Adrian's plan. "I'll have Rhys book a hotel for me. I think that might be best."

"As you wish. We'll see you soon, cuore mio."

The call ended, and I set my phone next to my now-cold coffee. The son of a bitch had not only roped me into a hunt I didn't want, but he'd ruined my morning decompression time. From anyone else, that would have been grounds for a friend-ship divorce. The only reason he got away with it was because I owed him my life about a hundred and seventy-five times. By last count.

With another groan, I pushed myself out of my chair to pack and mentally prepare myself to face a nest of edgy vampires. But as I rose to my feet, a looming shadow lurched out of my room.

2

Katerina

MY HEART CRASHED against my ribs. I summoned fire into my palms and winced as the heat spread up my bare arms, unchecked by the runed gloves I usually wore when I handled my magic.

I readied myself to launch a fireball at the figure's head… but as the shadow stepped into the rising pre-dawn light, I reversed my heat and turned the ball of flame into a hunk of ice that cracked against the patio.

Sucking in a breath, I slapped my hand to my chest. "Rhys Byrne, what the ever-loving—"

My words dried up when I caught sight of his eyes, as white as I was sure my face was right now.

"Whispers." His voice was detached and emotionless as

he relayed whatever vision his second sight had forced on him. "Whispers in their heads telling them to act. To fight. To protect. A city on the edge of war. Blood versus blood. A balance slipped."

His lanky six-two frame wobbled on unsteady legs, and I rushed to catch him and direct him into one of the chairs before he fell. I knelt beside him, my hand on his arm, and waited until his eyes cleared to their usual vibrant green.

"Hey, you." I did my best to keep my tone light while his mind returned from its jaunt to the future. "Want to tell me what you saw?"

I hated the necessity of pushing him as he came out of his daze, but his mother and I had learned that if we didn't catch him right away, more details got lost. His second sight was weak, coming infrequently and without warning, and we were still trying to figure out the best approach to help him through it.

For better or worse, Rhys was so eager to help me, he didn't seem to mind.

"A fancy house? White columns. Beautiful people. And another group that looked like they were in pain. Clutching their heads, upchucking all over the place." His lip curled in disgust. "Now there's an image I'll be carrying around in my head for a while. There was darkness. Like the whole world went black. Don't really know what that was about. I saw you, Adrian, Barrett. You were standing around… well, me, I think."

Shit.

We must have reached the unfortunate conclusion at the same time because the last of his haze disappeared and his eyes lit up. "I'm going with you."

He said it with far more excitement than the situation called for. Although he'd been a part of my world since the day he was born—his mother having been with me since the day *she* was born, and so on and so forth—there was so much he had yet to learn. As a budding Seer, he stood on the fringes of the community. Barely a toe dipped into the rapid current where one wrong step would send him hurtling towards a waterfall of magic and chaos and potential death.

Maera and I had done our best to explain it to him, but our warnings hadn't quenched his desire to wade deeper. If anything, they had spurred him on. I suppose we should have seen that coming.

"Your visions aren't written in stone," I reminded him. "I could leave you behind, and the next one would be different."

The brightness in his eyes dimmed as his shoulders hunched. "You wouldn't. Kat, come on, you promised. You're supposed to be teaching me. And something about that vision… I get the sense it's important I'm there. For my sake, if not for yours. You can't leave me behind."

Damn the kid and his doe-eyed expression that made it so difficult to turn him down.

"You'll have to get permission from your mother. I don't care if you are eighteen, you do not step foot in my car without her say-so. She scares me more than I respect your legal rights." I shuddered at the thought of yet again incurring Maera's wrath for letting Rhys get wrapped up in my work. "And if she does say yes, you will follow my instructions to the letter. If I tell you to sit in a snowbank, you will drop your ass into that snow and stay put until I say you can get back up."

He just about wriggled in his seat like a puppy who'd just heard the word *car.* "You got it. Absolutely."

I heaved a sigh and shoved my hand through my hair. "Don't get your hopes up. Your mother will never agree to this."

Thirteen hours later, while Rhys got settled in his half of our hotel suite, I dropped my overnight bag on the queen-size bed I'd claimed as mine.

The rooms were nice enough. Large windows overlooking the quaint streets that made up Orillia's downtown. Light furniture, soft grey walls, a massive television in the living room for all the time I didn't intend to spend there.

Maybe when this was over, I would come back for a real visit.

If the city still stood by the time I was finished.

From what Adrian had told me when he'd called back to

give me the details, the large house the nest called home was on the outskirts of the city. Staying there might have proved smarter than being downtown in case our hunt for the queen devolved into a flaming trash heap, but there were benefits to me staying as far as possible from the vampires. Being in the middle of them—my discomfort aside—would make it more difficult to see the big picture. Adrian and Barrett could be my eyes and ears within the nest, but if someone was stirring up trouble, I wanted to keep my attention on the city.

Once my few effects were stashed in the dresser, I pulled on my gloves. The leather stretched up to my elbow and ended at my first knuckle, leaving my fingers exposed. I'd oiled them recently, so the supple hide moved like a second skin, reassuring me that I would be prepared for anything I faced. The runes, etched with an old magical compound, helped me channel my power, keeping it focused in my palms so it didn't fly wild and damage anything I didn't want damaged. They were the only things I had with me from my mortal life, the leather imbued with extra magic that preserved it from the ravages of time and hard wear. I never went hunting without them.

As ready as I would ever be to meet with this Trillium person, I left the room, gathered Rhys from where he was pacing a hole in the white-and-purple area rug, and headed back to the car.

We were due to meet Adrian and Barrett a few hours after sundown, which in March was still early in the evening, but I wanted to get to the nest with enough time to scope the place out and get a feel for the house's magic.

Adrian had mentioned something strange was going on with the human thralls. I hoped to see it for myself before I stepped inside and experienced it firsthand. I didn't deal well with people at the best of times, which usually led to Maera lecturing me on how not to respond when irritated, so it was better if I took time to prepare.

"If you have any visions, let me know," I said to Rhys as I pulled up across from the house and put the car in park.

"I can tell you right now this is the house I saw." He hunched down in the passenger seat as though it would stop anyone walking by from noticing his flaming red hair and handsome face. "The columns, the porch. There are more columns inside. It's like a movie set or something."

"That's vampires for you. Some of them love to live up to the hype."

Rhys snorted, but his smile faded quickly. "If this is the house, should we really be so close to it? Based on what I saw, we know it's not going to end well." He frowned at his shoes, no doubt thinking about the upchuck detail.

"Believe me, the last thing I want to do is step foot inside that house. Have I ever told you about the first time I dealt with a vampire queen?"

Interest lit up his green eyes. "You have not."

"She nearly ripped my head off, so I zapped her so full of lightning she burst."

"Cool." He drew out the word, and my ego danced under his awe. His fascination with my stories was one of the many reasons I kept the young Seer around.

True, that fight with the vampire queen had taken place about eight hundred years ago, and I'd had many vampiric encounters—both good and bad—since then, but that one stuck out in my memory. After so long, the details were fuzzy, but a person never forgot the first time they electric-grilled a bitch.

"So yes," I continued, "given the opportunity to walk away, I would. In a heartbeat. Unfortunately, I love Adrian, and that means I'm stuck here, dealing with the weird-acting thralls bringing up their dinner all over the expensive hardwood and searching for a missing undead monarch. You in?"

He swallowed hard, and his skin turned a bit grey around his mouth, but he nodded. "I am."

We sat in silence and watched as no one entered or exited for two hours until Barrett's red SUV pulled up out front.

As soon as I stepped outside, however, magic tickled the back of my neck. Unfamiliar. Dark.

"Rhys, stay in the car," I said, and had only just closed the door behind me when a large man darted out of nowhere, grabbed me by the hair, and set a knife to my throat.

3

Katerina

BEFORE THE BLADE could break skin, I drew on my fire and rested my hands on his. A yelp cut through my ear as he let me go, but he punched me in the side of the face, and stars burst in my eyes as I hit the ground.

I pulled more deeply on my magic but had no time to release it before the man flew backwards into a tree.

I pressed gingerly on my cheek and scowled at the pain that lanced upwards into my skull. Bastard packed a mean punch.

"Are you all right, Katerina?" Adrian asked. He cupped my chin and tilted my head towards the streetlight. Crimson streaks cut through his dark eyes, and he bared his fangs as he turned towards my attacker.

"I'm fine." I rested my hand on his arm to keep him from

doing anything rash. "I could have handled that."

Adrian refocused on me, his mouth quirked in his usual barely there smile. "Of course you could have, but I didn't want to deprive myself of dealing with the person who wounded my dearest friend. Still, it's interesting that he attacked you so close to the nest. I believe he's one of the thralls we've been asked to help deal with."

While Barrett closed in on the dazed man, I rose to my feet and took a good look at Adrian under the glow of the streetlights.

It had been a while since I'd made it to Muskoka to see him. We didn't live that far from each other—hadn't since we met—but recently life had kept us apart, not helped by Adrian's increasing reclusiveness.

He looked good, though. Of course he did. The military bearing he'd maintained since his first death made it impossible for him to look anything but well put-together. His brown hair, styled in a side-part that swept to the left with a sort of messy charm, was thick and soft and dark enough to highlight the paleness of his alabaster complexion. Now that he'd calmed down, his brown eyes lacked the scarlet ring that circled the iris. He must have planned well for this trip and fed on the way here.

While most of him retained a sense of his ancient years, his clothing was modern. A grey dress shirt with sleeves rolled to the elbows to show off his toned forearms, and black trousers that hugged his muscular thighs.

Hermit or not, he was taking care of himself. Or at the very least, his thrall was taking care of him.

Barrett looked exactly the same as he had the last time I'd seen him. Broad chest, wide arms, wide legs, everything about him guaranteeing massive pain if anyone crossed him. His buzzed hair had begun to grow out, and I was surprised to see a few sprouts of grey among the dark brown. His dark skin appeared a touch sallow, another sign that all was not as it should be.

Sallow or not, he was a handsome devil, and in his black long-sleeved tee, black jeans, black boots, he looked ready to punch someone through the head first, ask questions later, so I wasn't too worried about him.

We turned back to my attacker as Barrett wrestled him to the ground, his thick biceps straining against his shirt. Without a single ragged breath, Adrian's thrall dropped the man onto his stomach and bound his wrists behind his back with a zip-tie, then grabbed him by the arm and jerked him to his feet.

"Should we bring him inside?" he asked Adrian.

Adrian cleared his throat, a delicate sound that covered—I suspected—both his amusement and no small amount of lust at the competent display. "That would be wise. Trillium will know what to do with him."

The sound of a car window rolling down drew my attention.

Rhys leaned his head out the window. "Can I come out now?"

A low-ranking vampire answered our knock, and we stepped into a foyer that was just as grand as the exterior. Rhys had been right about the columns. There were two spaced evenly across the wide expanse, white marble with carved stone vines encircling them, blooming into delicate nightshade blossoms.

Beautiful if cliché, but who was I to judge? I kept a basilisk fang on my living room mantel.

The floor was black marble to offset the white of the columns, and I caught the shimmer deep in the stone, as though I were walking among the stars. A nice effect. Not that the foyer needed anything else to make guests feel small and inferior. The ceilings had to be at least twenty feet high, and the sweeping staircase draped in crimson carpet added to the vibe of decadence.

A sideboard stood along the wall to my right on which sat five empty decanters. Why would they need so many? Different varieties—engineer versus artist? Different blood types? Just to look impressive?

While we waited for Trillium to join us, a vampire swept in from a room on our left. She wore a high-necked, sleeveless baby-pink dress that fell to her knees and hugged her ample curves, and her blonde hair was piled on her head and pinned with a pencil. Everything about her screamed *assistant*, an image supported by the tray she carried loaded with four empty glasses and a pitcher of water.

"Good evening, I'm Rose. Would you like anything to drink? We have blood available if you care to choose your selection. I'm afraid we don't have anything else besides water to offer just now—we've had no reason to stock our kitchen."

I drew in a deep breath on her behalf when it became clear she'd fallen off the habit herself.

"I'm fine, thank you," I said, and the others refused as well.

Rose set the tray on the sideboard. "Trillium will be with you shortly." Then she was gone, a veritable whirlwind.

A door opened at the top of the stairs, and a moment later, a woman draped in cloth of gold swept down towards us. Perhaps *floated* would be the better description. Were her feet even touching the floor?

I found myself staring at the hem of her dress, waiting for an opportunity to see for myself.

In another breath, she was directly in front of us. Her long brown hair flowed over her shoulders in waves that reflected the rich red highlights, and both hair and dress worked together to draw out the subtle golden notes in her brown skin. Her eyes were especially striking, the deep honey hue ringed with a crimson so bright it looked fake.

Someone had been neglecting mealtime.

Adrian bent over the woman's hand. "Trillium, it's lovely to see you."

"I thank you for coming," she said, her voice as honeyed as her eyes. "And that you came so quickly." She bared her fangs at the man flailing between Adrian and Barrett. "What gift have you brought me?" She stepped closer. "Harvey Weylon. I never thought you'd have the balls to cross my path again."

He thrashed harder, not seeming terrified at all by her not-so-subtle threats.

Until a moment ago, aside from the murder attempt, he'd been almost docile. In Trillium's presence, he acted like a rabid beast champing at the bit to drive his teeth into the vampire's neck.

Ironic.

"Take him downstairs," Trillium ordered. "We know how to deal with troubled thralls."

I frowned and stepped forward, fire drifting over my hands and up my arms. "And how is that exactly?"

Trillium eyed me from head to toe, irritation sparking in her expression and just as quickly fading into neutrality. Hiding her feelings or remembering who she was dealing with? "No harm will come to him, sorceress. Until we figure out what's wrong with them, we're keeping them contained. They're provided with sufficient food and water, blankets, a daily change of clothes, a shower—not that they're making use of any of it. They've been eerily non-responsive. The only difference from their usual accommodations is the heavy bars around their rooms."

I drew in my magic, extinguishing the fire, and fell back beside Adrian. I wasn't here to challenge or threaten these vampires unless I had good reason. From the story we'd been given, they were the victims, and for now, I would give her the benefit of the doubt.

"How many do you have contained?" Adrian asked.

Trillium's shoulders slumped. "Over a dozen." She gestured for two of her people to escort the thrall downstairs. Barrett handed him over with a wary eye, but the vampires didn't acknowledge him.

Once they were gone, Trillium nodded for us to follow her. "Come. This tale is best told sitting down." Her gaze flicked towards the stairs. "And with few ears."

4

Katerina

WHEN WE CROSSED from the foyer into the sitting room, I would have guessed we'd stepped in a whole other house.

Gone were the lofty ceilings and marble flooring, gone were the macabre decorations and refreshments. Thick cream carpet pressed under my boots, and by habit, I kicked them off and set them next to the door as the others followed suit. The furniture was darker than the pieces in the hotel suite, offset by warm off-white upholstery on the plush love seat and matching low-back armchair. A low, round coffee table was nestled between the seating, adorned with a floral centrepiece scattered with rich, velvety violets and sprigs of baby's breath.

The standout feature of the room, though, was the lack

of windows. Based on the elegant but comfortable decor, I guessed this was the queen's favourite space. Much like Adrian's library back home.

Trillium gestured for us to sit. Rose showed up just in time to drag two extra dining chairs from the corners of the room for Barrett and Rhys.

Adrian and I took the love seat, while the queen's second dropped into the armchair. Rose left again, shutting the door firmly behind her.

"The trouble began a month ago," Trillium started without any extra prompting. Her brown hair cascaded over her shoulder, flowing down to her waist, and as she crossed one perfectly toned leg over the other, I caught Rhys swallowing hard against the allure she exuded.

"We typically keep a rotation of a dozen human thralls in the house at any given time, with three to four dozen circulating throughout the city."

"For how many vampires?" I asked. The number of thralls seemed high for the number of vampires I'd seen here so far, which was four.

"Over a hundred," Trillium replied. "They don't all live with the nest, and not all of them need to feed often. Several of us are old enough to go weeks without a meal if we so chose."

Huh. A little more than four, then.

"Our thralls are treated well. They're paid, their medical

needs are attended to. We exchange blood once a year to ensure the bond remains strong, which boosts their strength, speed, senses, and healing. In return, they volunteer themselves for our wellbeing and see to our needs. You've noticed Rose acting as a servant? That's not her usual position."

Could have fooled me.

"For all the advantages they enjoy, however, not all thralls are suited to the role. Some humans don't react well to the frequent blood loss, even minor as it is—by rule in this house, before you ask—or to the shift in sleep schedule that's required to accommodate us. A few times a year, we have to let one go. So it seemed unfortunate, and somewhat inconvenient, for us to say goodbye to four in the same month, but not alarming."

Her blood-ringed eyes shot to the door, then back to me and Adrian. "When we caught one spiking the blood with tap water, we knew there was something seriously wrong. With the bond in place, they shouldn't have been able to harm us."

Rhys frowned in confusion. "Water would harm you?"

She barely spared him a glance. "We can stomach blood but nothing else. Tap water has chlorine, lead, unfiltered pharmaceuticals—all kinds of things our bodies can't process. It wouldn't have killed us, but it would have made us ill and left us weak until we could feed again. Fortunately, she was spotted. There's always the chance we would have scented the change before we drank, but there's no guarantee. The human involved was questioned but said nothing. She was the first to be put in the cells."

"Very generous of you," Adrian said, picking at a speck of invisible lint on his pantleg.

She narrowed her eyes at him. "You know Her Majesty, Adrian. She has strict rules in this house, and she enforces them. None of us would go against her."

"Where is your queen?" I asked.

Trillium's lip twitched. "I'm getting to that. Not a week after the blood incident, one of the sleep rooms caught fire. These rooms are in the middle of the house, much like this one, with no windows and only one door, which was barricaded. It was midday. We lost one of our own, but I'm grateful we had warning enough and didn't lose more."

"My sympathies for your loss," Adrian said, inclining his head.

She acknowledged his sentiments with a bow. "We caught the humans who did it. Three more thralls working together. At this point, we attempted to renew the blood bond with several of them. They didn't respond well, and the results were… unappetizing."

Rhys and I exchanged a glance. Upchucking.

"We had no choice. We released all of them from their bond. None of them could be trusted. Some argued and insisted they be allowed to stay, but we couldn't take the chance. Something—or someone—had blocked their bond. Was controlling them. They left and everything seemed to calm down. Until five days ago when Her Majesty disappeared."

Her expression shuttered, and I wondered if that was the end of her cooperation. Was the rest too confidential? Too incriminating?

I looked to Adrian, happy enough to let him take the lead on vampire politics. His face remained neutral, as though he were ready to wait as long as it took without any hint of impatience or curiosity. I did my best to do the same, but before long, I had to bite my tongue to keep my questions to myself.

Rhys fidgeted in his seat while Barrett seemed to have become one with his chair.

Finally, Trillium's eyes cleared. "She was sitting in this very room. Most of us were out of the house. The only people here were her most loyal servants. I was supposed to be home that night, but I had last-minute plans."

Feeding, most likely. With the thralls gone, the vampires would have been strapped for blood. I wasn't about to push the issue, though. My purpose wasn't to start a diplomatic war over vampire consent.

Not yet anyway.

"All hell broke loose when Rose came in to refill Her Majesty's glass and found the front door open and the queen gone. Her cup had spilled across the floor, and there were scraps of torn fabric on the chair. We did our best to follow the scent of the people who took her, but while there were definitely humans among them, their trail went cold not far from the house. There was also a hint of something… other."

Adrian's nostrils flared. "Confirming vampiric involvement?"

The second's honey-crimson eyes flashed. "What other explanation is there? Her drink might have been drugged, but if she was too weak to put up a fight, why were her clothes torn? If she was at full strength, how could a bunch of human thralls have wrestled her out the door without anyone in the house hearing?" She turned her gaze on me. "You understand why we asked you to come in. We need someone impartial to investigate. At this point, we can't even trust our own."

I did understand. While I was no happier about it now than I was when Adrian first called me, I saw why I was their best choice.

Rhys cleared his throat, and when everyone looked his way, his face flushed as red as his hair. Despite his embarrassment, he asked, "Did you hear any of the thralls talk about voices? Whispers?"

Pride surged through me that he was stepping forward with questions of his own, and it sparked my irritation when I caught the way Trillium stared down her nose at him. "You mean rumours? Conspiracy?"

The young Seer squirmed. "More like mental manipulation?"

"I can't say I did," she said, and turned an exasperated glance on Adrian.

Adrian, however, did not rise to Trillium's bait of talking down to the mortals. "Mr. Byrne is blessed with second sight. I believe he's referring to a vision he had about your situation."

Interest flickered in her eyes, and she switched her attention once more to Rhys, giving him a thorough appraisal. "Whispers, you say? Whispers could be commands from their new master. A weak telepathic link forms during the bonding process. If we had any doubts that one of us was behind the abduction, you've cleared them. I thank you." She smoothed her skirts, uncrossed and recrossed her legs, and refocused on me. "What is your plan, then? How do you intend to find our queen?"

My least favourite part: being put on the spot.

Did I have a plan? Of course I did. That plan was to question one of the rogue human thralls until they told me something useful. When that failed, I would attempt to go through the vampires. One of those groups knew where their queen was, and one of them would talk. Even if I had to start a few fires to make it happen.

"I'd like to start in your dungeon," I said.

Trillium looked disappointed by my practical response, but she nodded. "I'll make sure you're granted access, though I doubt you'll get much out of them."

"If they're being controlled by a new master, I'd like to at least rule out the possibility they'll tell me who it is."

"I hope you have more ideas than that, Ms. Palon. Without a queen at the head of this nest, my power only extends so far. There are already some here considering the option of challenging me for my position, and if they succeed, the fate of this city will be in question."

5

Katerina

To no one's surprise, Trillium was correct. None of the thralls gave up anything beyond dark glares. My pal Harvey went so far as to offer a silent threat, but nothing useful.

At least it appeared Trillium had told the truth. The prisoners' accommodations were more than adequate.

On that cheery note, Rhys and I returned to our hotel.

It was closing in on four o'clock in the morning, but Adrian and Barrett escorted us back so we could speak privately and devise our strategy.

"I'll do my best to get a feel for the vampires once we're back at the nest," Adrian said as he settled on the cushy cream couch. Barrett sat beside him. "Though, if Trillium is right and there are challengers for her position, it might be difficult to differentiate between the tensions of natural competition and those of a coup."

I huffed and started the kettle for tea while Rhys stood staring out the window. He looked exhausted, but to his credit, he never complained. Overnighters were a rough but regular part of the whole "keeping the world in balance" gig.

"Does this queen have a name?" I asked. "Or is that taboo? Is she above such lowly conventions?"

Adrian laughed, his fangs flashing in the soft light of the table lamp. "While etiquette does encourage people to use her title, I've avoided her name to prevent confusion. It's Orillia."

"Named after the city?"

"Or the city named after her." He shrugged. "There's some question about how far back she goes, and this city is steeped in unknown history."

"All right, so. Orry is sitting in her comfy chair, pulling an Adrian with her feet up, and in waltzes a bunch of biters and thralls who ruin her nice outfit and haul ass out the front door. No one hears it happen. Red flag number one that someone in the house is involved. Next, a group of loyalists—we assume—attempts to hunt the thralls and loses them. This tells me the humans were sent in as a distraction and were likely killed by their new master to ensure the trail stays cold."

Adrian looked grim. "I think that's a fair assumption."

"All that to say, I agree with you. The sun will be up in a few hours, which makes you useless to me" —I blew him a kiss to take the sting out of my quip— "so yes, you take the vampire angle for now and see what you can learn. Barrett, Rhys, and I can take the thralls. If the ones in the basement won't talk, maybe we'll have luck with the ones still walking around. We'll see how many are breathing to start."

"I'll be here at first light," Barrett said.

I wrinkled my nose and leaned against the counter in the tiny kitchenette. "Please, no. At least give me a chance to have a coffee before I spend the day with you. Let's say nine o'clock. Early enough to catch them awake if they're on vampire time, late enough that I'm less likely to set them on fire for being uncooperative."

Barrett frowned, no doubt unimpressed by my lack of get-to-itness, but to hell with him. He wasn't the one who had to deal with his grumpy face.

"Rhys, can you tell me more about this vision of yours?" Adrian asked.

Rhys left the window, dropped into the chair across from the couch, and propped his socked feet up on the edge of the coffee table. "Most of the details have already faded, so I might need Kat's help to remember all of it."

I left the water to boil and joined Adrian on the couch. Barrett was either offended by my closeness or believed some-one had to be standing to prevent the world from ending because he got up and took his position behind Adrian. Always on alert, this one. I found it incredibly sweet.

Step by step, Rhys took Adrian through everything he remembered, with very little nudging from me. His retention had improved considerably over the past few weeks. Soon, I suspected, he wouldn't need to rely on witnesses at all.

When Rhys finished, Adrian tapped his thumb against his lips, lost in thought for a good long while until the younger man began to fidget.

"I'd like to try something with you, Mr. Byrne. An exercise you might want to practice to improve control over your ability. If you're willing to play guinea pig."

Rhys shot me an alarmed stare, and I smirked. "You're the one who wanted to come with me because you thought it would be important. Maybe this is why. You can trust Adrian not to hurt you or make you cluck like a chicken. Any idea of his is usually based on solid theory."

Rhys nodded, still looking unsure, and Adrian gestured for him to come closer. Rhys pulled the chair across the rug until his knees brushed the vampire's.

"I wish I had my books with me," Adrian grumbled. "This is why I don't like leaving my library. There, everything I need is within easy reach. Instead, I'll have to go by memory. We'll start by taking a few deep breaths."

I laughed as memories washed over me of another time,

another voice telling me not to waste concentration on breathing. There wouldn't always be an opportunity to breathe in a fight.

My heart pinched, but I let the pain go. This was hardly the place for reminiscing. Emrick's lessons wouldn't help Rhys.

Unless the Seer suffered the same problem I had—the burden of too many expectations and not enough self-confidence.

I quirked an eyebrow and sat back in my seat, watching with interest as Adrian took Rhys through a few basic meditation techniques until the Seer sat limp as a noodle.

"Good," Adrian said softly. "Now I want you to find the place in your mind where your visions tend to come from. How does it feel when they come on? Where are they focused? Imagine tickling that spot with your finger, waking up those nerves."

Rhys's lips twitched with a smile, and I held back a laugh, not wanting to know what he was thinking.

"When you do that, do you notice anything about what goes on in your mind? Does focusing on that spot trigger any emotions or thoughts you associate with your visions?"

"It feels… weird," Rhys murmured. "Like the rush of blood in your ears when you stand up too fast. Or that itchy feeling in your nose when you need to sneeze."

That didn't sound comfortable at all. No wonder his second sight took so much out of him.

"Excellent," Adrian said. "Keep focusing on that spot. Imagine yourself burrowing into it. I suspect you instinctively keep that section of your mind closed off to protect yourself, to not be overwhelmed by a constant influx of information. The result is that it takes an extreme, intense vision to push its way to the surface. Without practice, without knowledge, the rest of your brain has no way to process what it's seeing, so you forget the details and your body needs time to recover. I believe that with effort, with patience, with practice, you can make the visions come naturally. If not at your beck and call, then with much greater ease."

Rhys's breath quickened, and his eyes shifted beneath his closed eyelids. His hands clenched and unclenched on the armrests.

Worry screamed at me to go to him and make sure he was all right, but Adrian's relaxed posture kept me in my seat. My friend was far from all-powerful or all-knowing, but after so many years, he had a good nose for trouble.

When Rhys's eyes snapped open, milk-white washed out the bright green, and I watched, fascinated. Had he really triggered a vision with a bit of breathing?

I wished Emrick were here to see it. I would have loved to rub it in his face.

I retracted that wish as the room's temperature dropped. My heart lurched, my palms grew clammy, and all my suspicions about the change in atmosphere were confirmed when Rhys's empty voice spoke up. "Death in the mist. Danger, pain, tears."

Yep, that sounded about right.

I sank into the couch and sighed in resignation as a soft grey mist formed in the middle of the room and my blond-haired, silver-eyed, body-of-a-god ex-lover stepped out of the afterlife into my hotel suite.

6

Emrick

I WALKED INTO a comfortable scene in a cozy hotel room. The orange glow of the streetlights flowed through the parted curtains to my right, highlighting the back of the chair where Katerina's protégé sat with his white eyes focused on me.

Unnerving, but I'd seen Rhys in his vision state before, so I only needed a second to shake off my discomfort and take in the way Adrian leaned towards him, his expression intent, excited.

I wondered what I'd missed. The only thing that excited my old friend these days was experiencing something new, a rarity considering how much he kept to his library.

Barrett watched me from behind the couch, as stern and stoic as ever. Never mind that as a servant of Death I was more a staple of the universe than a supernatural being. In his opinion, I was magical enough to be lumped in with the rest and therefore deserved that baleful glower.

Finally, my attention landed on Katerina, and everything else in the room faded. Her ocean-blue eyes were cold as they rested on me. She crossed her arms, crushing the folds of her dark green sweater. Black leggings hugged her toned legs, and I hid my smile at the bright blue socks that peeked out from underneath. The woman was a creature of comfort. One of the thousands of reasons I loved her.

One of the thousands of reasons we were no longer together. I would have sacrificed so much more than my soul to keep her in comfort, and she couldn't forgive me for it.

My heart pinched as it always did when I thought of what we used to be versus what we were now. Seventy-five years apart after over eight hundred together, and instead of getting easier, as I'd expected it would, the separation had gotten harder. The bond between us, the tether that kept her tied to this world, was as strong as ever, and it anchored me to her in a way that prevented me from moving on. Time stretched out like a taffy pull, unbearably slow, taunting me with its infinite span and no possibility of a reprieve—or a return to where we'd been, living our endless lives together.

I swallowed hard and pulled my shoulders back, reminding myself why I was here, which wasn't to pine after the love of my eternity.

"We have a problem."

Kat snorted and waggled her foot. "You say that as if you didn't find the four of us in a room far from either of our homes, one of us in the middle of a vision, after we've just come back from a debrief with the Orillia vampire nest."

I looked to Adrian, who sat back on the couch and crossed his ankle over his knee. "She speaks the truth, my friend. If you've come to tell us the deaths have started to mount in this city, I believe we're a step ahead of you."

I felt deflated, but what had I expected? That I would run in with bad news and Kat would throw her arms around me in gratitude for opening her eyes to the issue? Because that had worked out so well last time.

"Good," I said. "I'm sure the shifters will be relieved to know someone is looking into it."

Kat frowned. "The shifters?"

I paused and lowered my hand from raising the mists, letting them drift away. "Isn't that what you're talking about?"

Adrian and Kat exchanged a look, then both of them turned to Rhys. The redhead had slumped into his chair, his chest rising and falling with even breaths.

Kat cursed and pushed herself off the couch. Her sweater fell just past her hips, giving me a perfect view of her curves, and her long black hair swung in heavy waves halfway down her back, familiar and hypnotic.

"Trillium didn't mention anything about shifters," she said.

"She might not know," Adrian said. "The pack and the nest don't mingle often. They live on opposite sides of the city, and they do their best to stay out of each other's way."

"No tensions?" Her voice was filled with a skepticism I understood. Feuds between vampires and werewolves were common; both species were incredibly territorial.

"Orillia and the shifter alpha—Terry—formed a truce decades ago. Clear borders across the city enforced and respected. They haven't had trouble since."

"If only more nests and packs could keep things so civil," Barrett grumbled as he shifted his weight on his feet.

"It'd make lots of lives easier," Kat agreed. "And less dead." She propped her hands on her hips and stared at my shoes. "What do you know?"

"Only what I saw after the fact," I said. "There have been three deaths so far. Poison in each case."

Barrett frowned. "A coward's method."

"In human form?" Kat asked. I nodded, and she looked to Adrian. "Coincidence?"

"That the nest and the pack have both been targeted? Unlikely."

"What's going on with the nest?" I asked. I couldn't help myself. I was limited in what I could do to help without risking

Kat's wrath and another fragment of my soul, but curiosity and my need to ensure Kat's safety refused to let me walk away now that I'd delivered my message.

Understanding flickered in Kat's eyes, but her tone was dismissive as she said, "Kidnapped queen, hijacked thralls—the usual drama. If the dead shifters are connected, though, a few more pieces fall into place. Do you know what level they were?"

"By the size of them? Enforcers, I'd guess."

She bobbed her head as though the answer didn't surprise her. "If Orry and Terry have an agreement, some degree of protection or alliance is probably included on both sides. Poison isn't a direct challenge. It's subtle. Whoever's behind this is looking to keep the shifters out of the fight, not draw them in. With the queen being taken, the shifters might have offered to help. Now they're distracted."

I didn't like where this conversation was going. Over the past nine hundred years, Kat had dealt with worse conflicts than a turf war in a small city, but that didn't make me any more comfortable with her being in the middle of it. Her magic wasn't nearly as strong as it used to be, which would leave her vulnerable if the situation devolved into battle.

But I wasn't about to suggest she sit this one out. The harder I pushed, the harder she'd push back, and I didn't want her rushing into anything just to spite me. So I swallowed my warnings and listened as the only two people in the world I cared about calmly discussed a brewing war.

"Think it would be worth talking to the shifters?" she asked.

"I doubt they'll talk to anyone right now," I said, breaking my rule of thirty seconds ago to keep my mouth shut. This woman drove me to the brink of madness. "From what I over-heard, they're locking down. No one in or out of their wards. No exceptions."

Kat scowled. "Of course, because why would they make it easy? I could try to force the issue, but I'll have more luck if we can bring the poisoner to their door. It would be good to know what sort of poison was used. Are we including witches in this growing mess, or was it your basic over-the-counter death from the hardware store?"

Unfortunately, I couldn't answer that question. My duty was to escort souls into the afterlife and leave them at the river to wait for whatever came next. I didn't know the how or the why of their deaths.

"Would it matter?" Barrett asked.

Kat leaned against the edge of the kitchen counter. "Maybe not. If it were important, Rhys would have seen something." Her gaze flicked to the sleeping Seer, and her eyes glazed over as her thoughts slipped away, but she brought herself back with a shake. "Unless something pops up that proves us wrong, let's assume the thralls poisoned the shifters on behalf of their new master and stay focused on them." She raised her chin and finally deigned to look me in the eye. "Thank you for this information, Emrick. It can only help to know more."

A clear dismissal if ever I heard one, no matter how badly I wanted to ignore it.

Rhys groaned, and his eyelashes fluttered. Concern flashed across Kat's face as she moved towards him, but before she reached his side, he sat up with a jerk, his eyes still a stark white. "Don't answer the door."

No one had time to ask what he'd seen before a knock sounded at the suite.

Adrian rose to his feet at the same time Barrett drew his knives. Centuries of habit moved me towards Kat, but she stepped away, fire pulsing over her hands.

For a breath, we stood still, waiting, hoping whoever was in the hallway left without trouble.

With the next inhale, chaos reigned as the door burst open and a dozen armed humans poured into the room.

7

Katerina

STILL REELING FROM Emrick's arrival and the shifter bomb She'd dropped in my lap, it took me a second to process the influx of strangers filling my previously cozy hotel suite.

All twelve carried knives and were ready to use them if their swiping and stabbing were anything to go by. Their expressions were hard, twisted with wild determination, but their eyes... they didn't seem to see us at all.

As they swarmed in, I stepped in front of Rhys and pumped more fire into my hands. He was still out of it, so I couldn't stuff him in a room, which meant my greatest priority had to be keeping these people away from him.

And ending this fight quickly. The hotel had been quiet when we checked in, but that didn't mean the noise of fifteen people brawling wouldn't draw attention.

Adrian leapt at the closest woman and took her to the floor. By the spray of red blood that splashed over the beautiful couch, I took our attackers to be human, which made me ninety-eight per cent sure they were thralls.

Who the hell had sent them?

I reversed my fire, drew ice spikes into my hands, and hurled them at the two men running towards me with their knives raised. One lodged in Man One's throat; the other hit Man Two in the chest.

Guilt squeezed my heart as the light dimmed in their eyes, but I shoved it aside. Rhys's life mattered more than my conscience.

Three were down, and the other nine had gathered around Barrett as the only non-magical in the room. He was doing an impressive job of fighting them off, but there was only so long he could keep it up.

Adrian launched himself into the mob, and they scattered. Four came towards me, spreading out as if they thought that would keep them safe. Either they had no idea who they were dealing with, or their orders overrode any sense of self-preservation.

Emrick pulled off his gloves and stepped forward, ready to turn the closest one into dust with his touch, but I barked his name to get his attention. These people were mortal, which meant a no-go for him.

He shot me a dark look, but I glared back harder until he scowled and disappeared into the mist. As soon as he was gone, I summoned more ice spikes and threw them two per hand. Three hit their targets as the fourth lunged at me and knocked me to the floor. Her knife dug deep into my shoulder, and I hissed through my teeth at the white-hot pain. She pressed her weight into me, pushing the blade deeper, and my hands shook as I wrapped them around her arms.

Panting through clenched teeth, I worked to stay conscious and sent my magic outwards. Frost crept over her black shirt, up her arms, across her chest. She stilled, and her empty gaze cleared, filling with confusion then horror as the frost thickened into a shell of ice that bound her arms to her sides.

I shoved her off as a scream cut through the room followed by a shout from Adrian. Rolling to my feet with a groaned curse, I spotted Barrett on the floor with a knife in his side. Three more thralls closed in on him. Adrian was too busy with another two to get to him, his fangs deep in the neck of one, his fingers curled into the shirt of the other to keep her in place. I left him to deal with them while I focused on the three attacking Barrett.

Pain wracked my shoulder as I launched more ice spikes, but my aim was true. One drove through a heart, another through a throat, and the third through a stomach. Mercy wouldn't allow me to leave that last one to die slowly, so I summoned one more spike and thrust it through his chest.

After a quick check to make sure Barrett was alive, I sucked in a gasp at the burn in my shoulder and turned to face the rest of the room.

Nine dead, Barrett down, me bleeding, and one bound thrall to contend with. Plus, no doubt, a manager debating the wisdom of sending the cops to find out what the hell we'd done to her hotel and a stinging repair bill I would charge to the nest for services rendered.

Out of breath and blinking through the black spots in my vision, I hugged my injured arm to my chest and plodded over to the woman I'd trapped. Her eyes were open, terror-stricken. I dropped beside her, watched her panic climb as Adrian tore out the throat of the last fighting thrall.

"Talk," I said.

"I-I can't." Her voice came out as a squeak, and I wondered where the woman was who'd broken down my door and stabbed me. This chick looked ready to burst into tears. Which, frankly, was insulting given I was the one with the knife sticking out of my shoulder.

On a deep breath, I yanked the blade free and dropped it on the floor beside me. Already, my flesh itched and prickled as it knit back together. I would have preferred to moan and groan in private, but thanks to this dickhead not spilling everything I needed to know, I had to stand here and appear indifferent.

Even Barrett had the freedom to make as much noise as he wanted, though I was impressed by the low volume of his complaints.

"Talk," I repeated.

"I can't tell you who sent me. The bond, it—"

I rested my good hand on her chest and drew more frost over my fingers. "At the moment, I don't give a shit who sent you. I'll find out soon enough. I want to know where Orillia is."

She frowned. "You're in Orillia."

"Goddammit. The vampire queen. Where is the queen?"

Movement beyond the thrall caught my eye, and I raised my head to find Rhys standing up. His eyes were clear if haunted, and they widened when they fell on the blood seeping through one of my favourite sweaters.

I was ready for him to collapse with exhaustion and horror, but his throat bobbed with a hard swallow, and he said, "I saw an old building. Crates and trunks. Crowds. A stage?"

A hiss escaped through the thrall's teeth, and I pressed my hand harder against her chest. "Where is that?"

When she didn't answer, I switched my ice for fire. The frozen cage encasing her melted, and sweat beaded on her brow, but her expression never changed. With a cry, she lunged to the side and, in a smooth, speedy motion, grabbed the knife I'd dropped on the floor and drove it into her heart.

I started back and cursed as the life drained from her eyes.

"Well, fuck me, I guess." My shoulders sagged in fatigue as I looked up at Rhys.

His face had grown even paler, and by the movement in his throat, I was certain he was trying not to vomit.

I leapt to my feet and stood between him and the corpse. "Hey, look at me." It took a few repetitions of his name before he raised his gaze to meet mine. "What else did you see? Focus on that, okay?"

He cleared his throat, and pride swelled in my chest at his attempt to stay strong. Accompanying my pride was the heat of anger at myself for putting him in this situation. At eighteen years old, he shouldn't have to be strong.

"There was that darkness again," he said. "I felt crushed. Like the world was closing in on me. I'm sorry it wasn't more."

I rested my hands on his shoulders and guided him across the room to remove him from the gore. "It's all right. You've done more than enough."

With a sigh, I turned around and took in the mess. The blood on the furniture, the floor, the walls. The broken door. The smashed end table. The dozen corpses were an especially nice touch. So much destruction in such a short amount of time.

At least my vision had cleared, which meant I was one step closer to being as good as new.

My attention landed across the room where Adrian knelt

over Barrett. "He going to live?"

Barrett's face was pale and sweaty, and his hands trembled where they helped Adrian press a cloth against his wound, but Adrian's expression was impassive, not a hint of worry showing.

"I believe so," the vampire said. "They didn't nick anything critical, but I'd like to get him patched up quickly. Shall we return to the nest before the police show up?"

I sighed and passed one last glance around. I'd been looking forward to having my morning coffee in this warm, welcoming space. Obviously that was out of the question.

And in another moment, Emrick would be back to turn these corpses to dust. As the thralls weren't magicals, he wouldn't be the one escorting them to the afterlife, but he would at least help us avoid the public relations nightmare.

I was nowhere near ready to see him again, so I nodded. "Give us a second to pack, and we'll go. I think it's time to have another chat with Trillium."

8

Katerina

BY THE TIME we reached the nest, it was nearing six o'clock in the morning.

Adrian and Barrett had been shown to their room where Barrett could get patched up, and Rhys had been escorted to another room to get some sleep.

That left me the only one standing.

So, as tired, cranky, and messy as I was, instead of winding down with a shower, I was back in the sitting room, staring down a vampire who looked seriously pissed.

At least it wasn't with me. Bonus.

"Whoever sent the thralls after you will pay," Trillium said.

"Of course they will. I don't let anyone push me around. But revenge plots won't help us. Yet. Does Rhys's description ring any bells for you? Stage, trunks, crowds, old building."

A light furrow formed between Trillium's eyebrows, doing nothing to mar her flawless features. "Maybe the Orillia Opera House?"

"Do you know anyone who would think of using it as a storage space?"

"It's a frequent haunt for many of us. Open late at night, easy to blend in, full of music and culture."

"And it already has a reputation of being haunted," Rose said as she topped up Trillium's cup with blood. She raised a water pitcher for me, but I shook my head. While there was a rogue vampire wandering these rooms, it wasn't in my best interests to consume anything they offered me.

Even without a coup, I'd think twice. The potential cross-contamination of beverages was a nasty concept.

"What about contenders for the throne?" I asked. "Has anyone expressed that level of dissatisfaction with Orillia's leadership?"

Trillium's eyes flashed at the casual use of her queen's name, but I didn't care. I wasn't one to bow and scrape because someone had a title. I'd had a few of my own over the years.

"*Her Majesty* is a fair and just leader." She sighed. "But of course, there are always those who believe they could do better. A year ago, we had a revolt among the ranks. A small group tried to take out those closest to Her Majesty, but they didn't get far. All of them are dead."

"You mean all the vampires who made themselves known are dead."

She nodded, conceding the point.

"What about their associates? Any vampires close to them you couldn't prove were involved?"

"Me," Rose admitted. "My mate, Dean, was one of the leaders of the coup trying to put another female on the throne. I didn't know what he was planning, or I would have stopped him. The fool. He was only a few hundred years old—what did he know of leading a nest? Her Majesty has done an admirable job keeping the peace with the Orillia shifters, keeping our thralls plentiful and varied, and allowing us to live without trouble so close to the city. It's everything most vampires could ask for."

She sounded sincere enough, but her connection to the previous revolt and the fact that she was the last person to have seen the queen set alarm bells ringing.

Then again, Trillium would have known about the connection, and she was now sitting pretty as acting queen. Sure, she put on a good show, but vampires were known for their poker faces.

"Anything more recent?" I asked.

Trillium shook her head, the scarlet ring around her eyes leaching into the whites. "Believe me, Ms. Palon, if we'd heard anything, we wouldn't need you."

I believed her.

I longed to sleep, but if there was a traitor in the nest, word would soon reach them that I knew Orillia's location. Every minute that passed risked her being moved.

My shoulder ached, my magic was low, and my body warned me that, immortal or not, I was in no state to handle any more nasty surprises, but I had to power through.

"A change of clothes and a ten-minute nap, and then I'll head to the opera house," I said, standing up and trying not to flinch at the pull of repairing flesh. "If all goes well, your queen will be back in her armchair by sunrise."

For those ten minutes, I slept like the dead.

An amusing comparison considering I was in a house filled with undead.

As I got dressed, I assessed myself and found all my injuries from earlier were gone, as though they'd never happened. Not even a hint of the knife wound remained.

The only confirmation I had that the attack on the hotel suite wasn't an unpleasant dream was that I was in a vampire nest. And that my heart still ached from my run-in with Emrick.

I thought I'd made myself clear that I didn't want to see him.

Which was a lie, of course.

I *wanted* to see him. To talk to him and share my thoughts and feelings. To feel his arms around me, his lips on my skin. I wanted to fight by his side and spend eternity in his company.

I loved him with all of my being, and all of my being was tied up in the bond that tethered me to him and to this world. Thanks to a ritual that had gone wrong, I existed because he existed, and now he would do anything to keep me with him. That was why he needed to stay away. As much for my sake as his.

Barely five minutes with me, and he'd almost killed a mortal to protect me. Did he want to become a wraith? Lose his memories, his passion, his *self* for the sake of rescuing me?

As if he didn't remember that was why we'd argued in the first place, because I'd figured out what was happening—what he was sacrificing to stay so involved in my life. Because I'd realized the colour draining out of him, lightening his blond hair, turning his tanned skin pale, were signs that he was fading.

His muscular frame, all broad shoulders and tapered waist, might stay the same, but what would they be to me if his hardened exterior no longer softened against me? If his silver eyes, like moonlight reflecting off water, no longer gazed on me with the depths of his love and desire?

The changes were subtle, barely noticeable to anyone other than Adrian or me, but after centuries of him being exactly the same, the shift was as striking as if he'd dyed his hair green.

Maybe it would take ten years for him to waste away—a

hundred, a thousand—it would still be too soon.

I couldn't bear the idea of being trapped on this earth without Emrick—*my* Emrick—existing here as well.

But I couldn't afford to dwell on my twisted feelings for that stubborn man. If I did, I would never find the focus to save Orry.

So I crammed Emrick into the trunk that lived in the back of my mind, locked it, chained it, ordered it to stay put, and finished getting ready.

Black leggings, runed gloves, crimson shirt in honour of the company I was keeping, then I left my room only to find Rhys stumbling, bleary-eyed and stubbly chinned, down the hallway.

"Shouldn't you be sleeping?" I asked.

He wiped his hand over his face. "Had to get up to get some water. Three visions in a day? Probably not a great idea."

"But you did it," I said. "You triggered one yourself."

His green eyes brightened with pride. "I owe Adrian a huge favour."

"I'm sure he'll collect in some strange way. Ask you to teach him how to use eBay or something."

I had to get moving, but before I left, I wanted to fill Adrian in on my plans and what I'd learned. If I didn't have backup, it was important someone other than the vampires knew where I'd gone.

We reached his room, and without my having to knock,

Adrian pulled open the door and waved us in.

"How did your meeting with Trillium go?" he asked in greeting before returning to his seat beside the bed. Barrett lay stretched out on top of the comforter, a sour look on his face and bandages wrapped around his bare torso.

Damn. The guy's muscles had muscles.

He was also breathing, which, strangely, came as a big relief. I would never admit I'd been worried about him, but I couldn't deny I'd stayed awake an extra few minutes hoping he'd be all right.

"Are we sure she's not responsible for everything?" I asked. "Call you in, have you investigate, and when you don't find anything, take over and move on?"

Adrian mindlessly rested his hand on Barrett's arm. "It occurred to me. I haven't seen anything to make me sit up and take notice, but that doesn't mean the signs aren't there."

"Keep an eye on Rose, too. Her lover was involved in an attempted revolt last year. Could be coincidence, but something smells off. She was also serving the queen that night, so it would have been easy for her to slip something into the blood."

"I'll see what I can find out." He frowned and looked at Barrett. "It will mean me going downstairs. Will you be all right on your own?"

Barrett set his hand on Adrian's. "I'll be fine. Or you can help me downstairs. We can work together."

Adrian flashed his fangs. "There's much we can do together, but only when you've rested and healed." He huffed and looked at me. "You're left going to the opera house by yourself, then."

"I can go with you," Rhys said, stepping forward. "You've got me using my second sight. I can help."

My stomach lurched at the thought of him walking into danger when I wasn't at my best to protect him, but I didn't have it in me to crush his confidence when he'd just started building it. I sent a desperate look to Adrian around Rhys's shoulder.

"I'd prefer you stay with me," Adrian said. "With Barrett injured, I could use another pair of eyes. Katerina will be all right, won't you, tesoro?"

"Of course I will be." I gave Rhys my most reassuring smile. "In and out, no fuss." He looked ready to argue, so I cut him off. "Maybe you can try to trigger a vision now? Something that will help me once I get there?"

Hope and self-consciousness battled in his expression.

"Come, Rhys." Adrian patted the foot of the bed.

Rhys sat down, closed his eyes, and followed the same breathing exercise Adrian had walked him through earlier. The three of us remained silent, watching him, waiting. The only sound was a faint drip of water coming from the adjoining bathroom.

After a few long minutes, Rhys's shoulders slumped.

"I guess I wouldn't be much help to you anyway. Nothing's coming. All I'm seeing is more darkness."

I set my hand on his shoulder and forced him to meet my eye. "You're no less important to me because you can't work your second sight on demand, all right? You're good enough as you are."

He nodded, but his disappointment was written across his face. I squeezed his shoulder, then stepped back. "I have my phone, so if you have any visions or you learn anything, text me. And try to get some sleep. For now, I have a date with an opera ghost."

9

Katerina

I'D NEVER BEEN to the Orillia Opera House before, and as I stood in front of the glass-paned double doors, the red brick glowing in the sunrise, I regretted that I hadn't.

One of the few joys I retained in this life was an appreciation of the arts. Theatre, music, hearing the same words and the same notes across centuries as social opinions shifted, as instruments evolved. *As You Like It* performed at the opening of the Globe Theatre in 1599 was not the same *As You Like It* audiences saw today even if the speeches remained untouched.

It was important to me to see that things could change even as they stayed the same. A reminder that I wasn't stagnant, either. That I could grow and adapt and not get stuck in the past.

Had Orry fallen into that trap? Adrian said he and the

queen often discussed the nature of immortality, but did that mean she embraced the constant rush of life, or had she rooted herself into a specific point in time, becoming a rock in the current? If she had, I understood why some of her nest might long for something different.

I hesitated on the front step, staring through the glass panes into the darkness of the opera house within.

Were we fighting for the right side on this? Just because Orillia had been queen for thousands of years didn't mean she should stay that way. The status quo wasn't always the best choice. Life was change.

But I trusted Adrian. He may have stepped back from the world, but he hadn't cut himself off from it. Through Barrett, through me, through his human servants who went out and lived, he made a point of adapting. Trends, slang, technology— even if he didn't use them, he always made a point to learn them. He thrived on novelty and never believed something was better just because it was old. If he believed Orry should keep her throne, I would side with him.

I could always change my mind later.

With that decision, I pulled opened the doors.

Inside, heat poured through the vents, combatting the early March chill with a bright, cozy ambiance. I wished I could stick around and explore, but I doubted the rebel vampires had stuffed the queen in a broom closet on the main floor. If she was anywhere, she would be in the basement. Probably some-where cold and damp, because of course I wasn't allowed to be comfortable on a hunt.

The administrative offices had only just opened for the day, which meant fewer people wandering the hallways. Lucky for me. Even so, while I searched for the stairwell, I kept my eyes open for any staff who might stop and ask who the hell I was.

Eventually I found the stairs and hurried down, stepping lightly to avoid any echo in the silent space.

At the bottom, I opened the door and walked into the impressively organized basement. Props, costumes, and set pieces mixed in with the regular fare you'd expect to see in storage. My housekeeper's heart would have been all aflutter over their labelling system.

Only the emergency lights were on, but I didn't bother to find the light switch. Instead, I summoned a tiny fireball and launched it above my head. The flame flickered and pulsed as it hovered, brightening my view enough to navigate the aisles of theatre life.

I crossed the length of the space, wandering the rows, searching for any sign of a crawlspace or storage room where a woman might be stashed. Halfway through my second tour, a soft thump caught my ear. I stopped where I was to try to pick up where it had come from.

For a long while, I was met with silence, but before I continued on my way, the sound came again. Weak. More like someone bumping furniture against a wall than an active knock, but the repetition made me more inclined to seek out the source.

Adrenaline coursed through me, heightening my senses, prickling my fingertips.

"Is anyone here?" I projected my voice just below a yell to avoid anyone upstairs hearing me.

The thump came again, still weak but insistent. I walked in the direction it seemed to be coming from, keeping my steps light, peering into the shadows. But there were no closed doors, no obvious places for anyone to hide.

My pulse rushed in my ears as I strained to pick up any sounds. Finally, the soft thump came again followed by a subtle scrape and what I swore was a soft murmur. It came from ahead of me until all of a sudden the direction shifted and the next thump came from behind.

Was someone messing with me? Was some motion-sensor prop reacting to my movements?

But when a soft scraping, like fingernails against wood, came from right beside me, I dropped my attention to a trunk on the floor. The damn thing had to weigh a tonne, even empty. It was easily five feet across, four high, made of heavy mahogany with metal bracings. The grooves in the carpet suggested it had been moved recently, and my heart lodged in my throat as the truth sank in.

A world of darkness, just as Rhys had said. He hadn't failed to trigger a vision earlier after all.

"Your Majesty? Orillia? Are you in there?"

The murmured voice came again, barely a whisper followed by more scratching. A prickle of rage spun through my blood, and fire flickered over my fingers. Staging a coup was one thing. Stuffing someone in a trunk was a whole other kind of warfare.

I knelt down and reached for the padlock, planning to reverse my fire so I could freeze the metal and snap it, when the glint of a knife flew into my peripheral vision. I dodged the blade, but before I could ready my defences, a heavy weight slammed into my side and knocked me to the ground. I reached up and lay my frozen hands on my assailant. A loud hiss vibrated in my ear. The weight disappeared, and I tried to scramble to my feet, but more hands grabbed me and pinned me down. I flailed my arms and legs against them, but even human—as I assumed they were by the time of day—they were too strong and too many.

Conscious of all the wooden set pieces, I summoned my fire and pushed outwards, letting the flames lick my palms and drift over my gloves. The people pressing on my shoulders jerked away, freeing me to throw a flame-wrapped punch into the face of a woman holding my leg. As soon as she let go, I used my free leg to kick the other guy in the chest. It took a few strikes, but his grip loosened as he readjusted, and I flipped onto my stomach. Embers burned into the floor, and I slapped my hands down to put them out before gaining my feet.

Five men and two women stared back at me.

I reversed my heat again and drew ice spikes into my palms. "Your master sent twelve of you to my hotel suite this morning. None of you made it out. That wasn't enough of a message about what happens to people who piss me off?"

A guy on my right snarled. "We got your message, but our orders stand. The queen stays with us, and the sorceress dies."

"Okay, good luck with that."

Knives flashed as the seven rushed me. I fought back, weaving and dodging their strikes, but they were fast, their speed and strength heightened by their master's blood.

One blade lodged in my lower back as another sliced through my arm, and I swallowed a cry as I jerked away to put my back to the wall. Not for the first time, I cursed my weakened magic. Two hundred years ago, I could have frozen this entire room within seconds, turning every one of these bastards into ice sculptures.

Time, heartbreak, and depression had worn me down, and only in the past couple of months had I begun to scrub off the rust. I doubted it would be enough to take down all seven.

Not that I would make it easy for them.

Blood spilled down my arm, and my fingers went numb, making me drop one of my ice spikes. I tightened my grip on the other one and returned their attacks with a few of my own. The spike pierced a man's forearm as he charged me with his knife raised, and when he dropped his weapon, I set my hand against his chest and absorbed his heat until he collapsed to the ground, dead. The others circled me, but I held them off by wrapping fire around my good hand. Pain throbbed in my injured arm and along my spine, sending nausea gurgling through my guts.

Weak magic or not, I fought the urge to blast outwards with my fire. It would end this fight quickly, but I couldn't risk burning Orillia in her trunk.

One of the women wasn't put off by the fire. She closed in and tackled my legs. I managed to keep my feet, but the distraction left me vulnerable to the man who charged my other side, taking the three of us to the floor.

I reached for more magic, and horror gripped me when I found it circling, waning. I had enough juice for one more assault, so I would have to make it count.

The two thralls set on me with their heavy boots, railing me in the ribs and head with their steel toes. The others joined in, giving me no chance to guard myself against their kicks as they battered me to the edge of consciousness.

Stars burst in my vision, and I knew I had moments before darkness consumed me.

Pushing through my foggy thoughts, I latched on to the

magic swimming in my core. Fire came easily to me, ice just as much, but if I wanted to put these people down, I needed something more targeted. It would risk the building, but at this point, it was me or culture. Between this place and the hotel, Orillia would be writing some hefty cheques once I got her ass back on her throne.

Teeth clenched, clinging to awareness, I tapped into the dryness in the air, and the zing of static electricity tickled my fingertips. With one last deep breath, I released the dregs of my magic and squeezed my eyes shut as the glow of a half-dozen lightning bolts shot from my palms.

Screams filled my ears. The reek of burned clothing and flesh and the scent of burning wood ravaged my nose. Shit.

My vision wavered, and I couldn't find the strength to sit up. The assault on my body had stopped, but I was past the point of dragging myself out of here until my body patched itself up. With my last ounce of effort, I reached for the fire spreading across the bottom of a scene backdrop. If it jumped from there to anything else, the odds of the entire basement igniting were too high. I rested my fingers on the edge of the wooden frame, winced as the non-magical flames kissed my skin, and sent frost over the surface.

The last ember flickered out as unconsciousness took me, and in my final moment of awareness, I noted a sudden drop in temperature.

10

Emrick

K AT LAY DRAPED in my arms as I stepped through the after-life and into her room in the vampire nest.

Her fingers were burned, and blood had soaked through the tears in her sweater, but as I watched, the blisters on her hands retreated, and the open wounds closed into angry scars that would be gone by this afternoon.

I didn't care how quickly she healed, I hated that she kept putting herself in situations where she got hurt. Especially when she went in without backup. And then she had the nerve to get pissed at me when I tried to help?

The woman would be the end of my sanity.

It was a miracle I had any left after nearly a millennium in her company.

I set her on the bed and brushed her dark hair out of her face. As I did, my bare finger caressed her cheek, and I shivered at the rush of energy that surged between us, thrilling my nerves, filling me with a flush of life that nothing else in this world offered me.

My touch should have killed her. No one else was immune to it. But she was a part of me, our souls as linked as our hearts once were.

I craved more, missed her with an ache that wouldn't abate, but I forced myself to pull my gloves on and step away from her while any strength remained to do so. Regardless of my wishes, I would respect hers.

Though that didn't mean I would stand by while she got her ass kicked again. The thralls were off limits to me, but nothing stood between me and the rogue vampires. They'd traded their souls for their unlife. Death had no claim on them, which meant there were no consequences for me in destroying them.

Kat groaned, and I shoved my hands in my pockets as I leaned against the wall near the door.

Her eyelashes fluttered, and her deep blue eyes landed on me as soon as they opened. The initial joy in her gaze at the sight of me warmed my chest and nearly brought me to my knees, but too soon it hardened into cold frustration, and the walls around my heart went back up.

"I guess I should thank you," she said.

I shrugged. "You put the fire out. You would have been fine. Left in an awkward situation if the staff had come down, maybe, but alive."

"I don't suppose you freed the queen?"

I blinked. "I didn't see the queen."

"She was in the trunk beside me."

Oops. "I guess she'll enjoy another day's rest, then."

Kat pushed herself up, winced, and rose unsteadily to her feet. It took all my restraint not to offer support. To strip her down and help her into the shower. To kiss her until her pale cheeks flushed red. I pressed my back against the wall to hold myself in place.

"Are you sure it was wise, going there by yourself?"

By the rage that flared in her eyes, I suspected kissing her would have been the lesser crime.

"Your history with vampires is… strained," I added.

To put it lightly. At least one vampire queen had almost ripped her head from her shoulders, and more than once, she'd been drained to the point of unconsciousness. There was a reason she'd put a moratorium on hunting them.

"I can handle myself, Emrick." She staggered to the dresser, pulled out her bag, and grumbled, "Though if I stay here any longer, I'm going to run out of shirts."

She pulled off her ruined sweater, and with her back to me, I saw the red, seeping knife wound close to her left kidney. My vision darkened. I was glad she'd dealt with the people who'd hurt her, because I might not have been able to hold myself back.

She threw the bloodied top in the trash and grabbed a sapphire-blue one to replace it. In another second, she was covered and walking towards the door. As she passed me, I slid my fingers around her arm and pulled her close.

Her breath hitched at the contact, her pupils dilated, and my body responded.

"I know you can take care of yourself," I said. "You've always been able to. That doesn't mean you have to." I swallowed hard and licked my suddenly dry lips. "You never have to be alone, Kat."

As she met my eye, I found myself swept into the current of her gaze. I could have stayed there staring at her for years and not grown tired of the sight.

Longing and pain slipped around the edges of her mask, and I held my breath, hoping her resolve would crack and she'd invite me back in. Her breath fanned against my collarbones, her lips parted, my heart stuttered.

Then she dropped her gaze, closing herself off from me, and eased her arm out of my grip to continue towards the door.

My chest heavy with disappointment, I prepared to step into the mist, but she turned and looked at me over her shoulder, her black hair cascading down her back in a midnight waterfall.

"Are you coming?"

11

Katerina

I SHOULD HAVE let Emrick go on his way, but the attack at the opera house had drained my confidence as well as my magic, and despite everything, I needed him beside me while I regained my strength.

So I led him down the hallway to Adrian's room, not bothering to knock when I got there.

Barrett was still lying down, though he appeared a bit more awake than a few hours ago. Adrian paced the room, and Rhys sat in the chair beside the bed. He still didn't look like he'd gotten much sleep.

On our entrance, Adrian stopped and gave me a questioning stare, his gaze flicking over my shoulder towards Emrick, but I ignored him. The nosy old man could wait until later to have his curiosity sated.

"How fond is Orry of enclosed spaces?" I asked as I dragged a chair from the corner of the room and dropped into it.

Emrick leaned against the wall, his hands behind him—his usual stance when around people to prevent any accidental contact.

Adrian raised an eyebrow. "She lives in a manor house, so I'd be inclined to say not very."

"And how bent is she on revenge, generally? On a scale of 'forgiving' to 'violence is my personality trait'?"

"I would place her somewhere in the middle unless pushed."

"Like being stuffed in a props trunk in an opera house basement?"

My friend's eyes flashed crimson, and he curled his fingers into talons. "They didn't."

"Unfortunately, I didn't get a chance to let her out before more thralls attacked, and she didn't make enough noise for Emrick to realize she was there. We'll have to go back, but…" I let out a resigned huff. "I can't go in alone. Not again. My own fault, really, for being such a respectful, sentimental sap, but I'd rather not burn down years of theatrical history if I can avoid it. And my magic is being stubborn." Barrett grunted, and I pretended to jump. "My goodness, Barrett, you weren't your usual chatty self, I forgot you were there. How are you feeling?"

He rolled his eyes, then flinched as his rippled muscles

flexed. "Better."

"Think you're up for another showdown?"

Adrian frowned. "Really, Katerina, I don't think—"

"And I don't think we have time. I'm sorry, Adrian. I know you're worried about him, and if he's not up to fighting, that's fine, I can go ahead without either of you, but the vampire queen of Orillia has been locked in a trunk while someone tries to take over her nest. If Trillium's not involved, what do you think her response will be when I tell her? What do you think will happen when we tell the shifters their people are dead because of vampire politics?" I looked at Rhys, who was sitting quietly, his green eyes fixed on me. "In your vision, you said the city was on the brink of war, and I think we're getting closer to that bugle call with every passing hour."

His bottom lip wobbled with nerves as he swallowed. "I haven't seen anything else, but something tells me you're right. I feel like I'm about to have another vision, standing just on the edge of it, and that's probably not a good sign."

Barrett wriggled his way up the pillows, eye twitching with every movement, and I pressed my lips together to hold back from telling him to stop. Adrian stood the best chance of keeping him from pushing himself too far, and I doubted even he had enough power to override his thrall's pride.

Once he sat up, Barrett took hold of the bandages around his stomach and peeled them back. The top layers were clean, but blood had soaked through the rest of them, and though the wound appeared to be healing nicely—and more quickly than should have been possible for a mortal—it was still open and seeping.

"Right. Okay. Barrett is a last resort only. Got it."

"To hell with that," he grumbled. "If I'm needed, I can fight through this. I've dealt with worse."

"And if you were all I had to worry about, I'd say cool, come with me and get yourself killed. But you belong to my friend, and he's tedious when he's grieving. So."

I crossed my arms and looked around the room. Once again, my options for help were sparse, leaving me with only my last pick of the team available. We couldn't afford to wait to get the queen out of the trunk. Barrett was about to keel over, Adrian was trapped inside until sunset, and Rhys…

Well, Rhys was a white-eyed zombie again. The approaching vision he'd sensed had caught up with him, so that was great.

He sat ramrod straight, his fingers curled around the edges of his chair. "Whispers demand blood." His voice held its usual detachment when bound by his second sight, but there was a note of urgency that caused a cold sweat to break out over the small of my back. "Two crowns fight for dominion at the height of the new moon. A nighttime serenade holds salvation, but only if the call is met."

He jerked as though he'd been hit and slumped to the side,

but Adrian darted over and caught him before he hit the floor. In a deft move, the vampire carried Rhys to the empty side of the bed. Barrett shimmied over with a series of wheezes to give the younger man space.

My heart took its time slowing down as I attempted to parse through this latest message. I watched Rhys, waiting for him to wake up and tell us more of what he'd seen, but his chest rose and fell and his body twitched with dreams. All these visions so close together had taken their toll on him.

"Nighttime serenade," Emrick repeated. "The opera house?"

"Maybe? I don't think so," I said. "The theatre's a holding space. If I'm right about how vampire politics works, the rebel queen needs to prove her position to the nest if she wants to take over, right?" When Adrian nodded, I continued. "That means she needs witnesses to Orry's death, and there are only so many vampires they can sneak into the basement without someone noticing. The stage itself could be an option, I guess—you vampires do love your melodrama."

"I don't see it," Adrian said. "They wouldn't be guaranteed secrecy from the mundane world. Security, staff. Anyone might walk in."

If the serenade didn't come from the location, what kind of saviour were we talking about? A resource? A relic? An ally? And what call?

Rhys groaned, and his eyelids fluttered open. "Ow."

Adrian poured him a glass of water, and I helped him sit up to drink it. His face was pale, his eyes haunted, and my soul ached as I said, "I hate to ask."

He waved me off and accepted the glass to drink on his own. "No, I know. I didn't see much else, though. Flashes of a big fight here in the house. People with long, sharp teeth popping out of nowhere. Not helpful in a nest of vampires, right?"

I pressed a kiss against his sweaty temple. "You did well. Don't be disappointed in yourself. Let's see if we can put the pieces together, okay?"

He nodded dully, and I pushed myself off the bed to pace, wishing my thoughts would settle so I could see things clearly. Everything was muddled. Twice now, the thralls had nearly gotten the better of me. If I didn't figure this out, the nest's problems would go from private to province-wide, and I'd have an even bigger mess to clean up. The clock was ticking, and the pressure weighed on me.

I had to break it down, talk it out. The answers were right in front of me—I just had to shift my perspective.

"You mentioned the whispers again. Trillium said the whispers are most likely the thralls getting orders from their master, so we can keep an open mind to interpretation, but let's set that aside for now. When is the new moon?"

Barrett grabbed his phone from the bedside table and opened the calendar app. "Tonight."

My chest tightened, and I did my best to breathe through the spike of stress threatening to overwhelm me. "All right, cutting it a little close, but we'll make do. What's next?"

"Two crowns fighting," Emrick said.

"That suggests Orry will be involved in some capacity. Either I'm about to have some good luck getting her out of that basement or someone is going to beat me to it and escort her here."

"Let's hope it's the former," Adrian said. "If it's the latter, it will mean she's too weak to fight."

"That brings us back to the serenade and a call. What sings at night that could help us?" I walked the length of the room and glanced at Rhys, hoping the question would trigger another detail for him, but he remained staring into his cup.

Emrick started. He dropped his arms to his sides and met my eye. "Wolves?"

Rhys's head jerked up. "Wolves. The people with teeth. You think they weren't vampires?"

The shifters.

"Well then," I said. "Rhys, I want you to stay locked in your room tonight, but I guess you have a role to play after all, Barrett."

"But—" Rhys started, and I shot him a look.

"Snowbank," I reminded him. His shoulders slumped in resignation, and I turned back to Barrett. "Not only do we need to convince Terry to hear us out, but we have to convince him it's in his pack's best interests to get their asses to the nest to fight with us." Saying it out loud, I appreciated how daunting a task it would be. "Better you than me."

Barrett snorted. "We'll have enough of a diplomatic nightmare on our hands with you being the one to save the queen."

"What are you talking about? I'm a perfect angel. She'll be thrilled to see me."

"As long as no other thralls are waiting for you," Emrick said roughly.

"That's why you'll go with her," Adrian said. "To ensure everything goes smoothly."

Although I'd already accepted the necessity of Emrick's help, I stiffened and averted my gaze from him. Adrian must have noticed, because he set his hands on his hips.

"If we want to live through this and settle tempers in this city, you need backup, and Emrick is all you have. You both need to get your heads out of your respective asses and work together."

I wrinkled my nose at his *dad* voice and reluctantly turned to Emrick. "Hands off the thralls."

His silver eyes flashed, and his jaw flexed, but all he said was, "Fine. But the vampires are mine."

12

Katerina

THE OPERA HOUSE wasn't nearly as empty as it had been during my first visit.

The lights were all on inside, the warm, welcoming glow spilling through the overcast afternoon. Snow had begun to fall, coating the concrete steps in a spattering of white flakes.

With the lack of sunlight, Adrian could have accompanied me, but it was too late to head back to the nest and insist that Barrett and I change partners. Instead, I stood next to Emrick, and the two of us assessed our position.

"It bodes well the place isn't surrounded by emergency vehicles," I said. "You got rid of the bodies?"

"All dust," he confirmed.

"Lucky them. Okay, I've counted six staff members so far.

You?"

"Four. I spotted them going in through that side door over there."

Not exactly a full house, but enough that I didn't want to risk walking in as I had that morning.

We'd driven here in my car. Emrick could have brought me through the afterlife, but for one thing, that would have involved touching him, and for another, we didn't know what condition the queen would be in when we found her, so having the car was the smart move.

Now, however, it seemed like physical contact would be necessary if we wanted to reach the basement unseen.

Resigned, I held out my hand. "Let's get this over with."

The corner of Emrick's lip twitched in amusement as he removed his glove and slid his fingers through mine.

The jerk of energy was immediate, slamming through my cells, buzzing along my nerve endings and waking up every minor sensation as my body slid through time and wound up right back where it was.

Contact with the spirit-herder was a never-failing rush, and I longed for more. I wanted his hands on me, his skin pressed against mine, filling me inside and out with the truth of my immortality, so wound up in him that I forgot everything else.

It never faded, this need for him, and it took the full force of my practical brain to remind myself why it wasn't possible.

I was saving him.

Saving myself.

If he stayed with me, it was only a matter of time before he no longer existed as the man I loved. So as difficult as it was to let him go, it was the only way forward. If I said it often enough, I hoped to one day believe it.

The mists swirled around us as we stepped through the afterlife, and by the time they cleared, we stood in the theatre basement.

The carpet was a little worse for wear, the backdrop singed around the edges, but the trunk was right where I'd last seen it. Instead of seven bodies on the floor, there were seven piles of dirt where Emrick had composted the thralls with his touch.

Excellent. A bit more work for the janitorial staff, but no city-wide emergency declared. Just the sort of clean-up I preferred.

I knelt beside the trunk, feeling much more protected this time with Emrick at my back.

Not wanting to push my luck, I worked quickly. Pulling in my heat, I cooled my hands so frost spread over the padlock. Layer after layer, it crept over the metal and up the mahogany panels. At least I didn't need to worry about accidentally freezing the queen to death. One of the perks of being undead.

Once the lock turned brittle, I stepped aside and let Emrick bring his heavy boot down on top of it, snapping the lock at the joint.

I flipped open the lid and cursed when I found the trunk empty.

Then I cursed a few more times.

"Looking for something?"

The smugness in the voice behind me created the urge to drive ice spikes into their eyeballs. I settled for drawing in a slow, deep breath and turned to face them.

A vaguely familiar vampire held the queen in his arms. She was conscious but unmoving, eyes open but unseeing. They'd obviously dosed her with something. Drugged blood? I hoped Adrian wasn't availing himself of any offered refreshments.

I summoned more ice into my hands, but all the vampire's vitals were blocked by the queen. Since my mission was to rescue her, I doubted anyone would appreciate me hurling stakes through her chest.

The vampire's lips peeled back in a creepy smile, and four more figures stepped out of the shadows beside him.

"Have you been waiting for me all day?" I asked in an exaggerated simper. "You *guys*, I'm flattered. But I'm afraid you got the wrong memo. I'm not here to dance."

I threw my ice spikes at the other four vampires. One hit home in a woman's chest, and she turned to ash where she stood. The other three missed. The vampires charged, but before they reached me, Emrick stepped through the afterlife and reappeared behind them. One staggered back, confused.

"Hey." Emrick winked and lay his bare hand on the man's face. The vampire had time to let out a gurgle of surprise before he crumbled into a heap of dust. One of the remaining two stumbled at the loss of their friend, and Emrick made quick work of her as well, leaving me alone with the last one.

My attack was interrupted when a human thrall stepped out from behind a backdrop and threw his beefy arms around my middle to pin my hands at my sides. I jerked to escape, but he squeezed tighter.

Before I could summon more magic, the vampire jumped at me and sank her teeth into my neck, only to pull back a moment later and spit my blood on the ground.

"Excuse me," I said through the echo of my racing heart. "Show some manners."

"What the hell is wrong with your blood?" the vampire asked. I wondered if she regretted those were her last words as Emrick rested his hand on the back of her neck.

The thrall squeezed me tighter, but I slammed my heel onto his instep, and when he flinched and jerked his foot away, I drove my elbow backwards into his sternum.

Emrick clenched his fists at his sides, but I gave him no chance to make any bad decisions before spinning around and pressing my frozen hand against the thrall's chest. I recognized my pal Harvey and only had a moment to wonder how he'd escaped his cell before the cold spread and the man's lips turned blue. A moment later, he fell, his heart still.

As one, Emrick and I turned to the vampire holding the queen. Now Orillia was on her feet, and the vampire held a stake to her chest.

After reacquainting myself with Harvey, this guy's face clicked in my memory. He was one of the vampires who'd escorted the thrall to the basement last night. One of the queen's supposedly loyal servants. How many other traitors lurked under her nose?

"Stop right there, or she's dust," he said.

I read the fear in his eyes, the desperation and confusion. He was the senior vampire here, and he had no idea what to do.

"You won't kill her," I said, drawing another ice spike into my hand as Emrick stepped into the afterlife.

The vampire searched for Emrick in the shadows and shifted so his back was against the wall. Smart man.

"Killing her will ruin the coup. Sure, she'll be dead and out of your hair, but you won't make it out of here, either. Your rebel leader will enter the race for the throne, but she'll have to contend with all the others who want it. Think she's up for it?"

Emrick reappeared close to the man, but he had no opportunity to lay a finger on him. Before he got close enough, Orry used the vampire's distraction to copy my moves. Weak as she was, she slammed her bare foot onto the guy's instep and slammed her head back into his nose. When he clapped a hand over his face, she spun, grabbed the stake out of his hand, and drove it into his chest.

I was impressed. Drugged as she was, she had oomph.

Now that she was awake and showing some unlife, I was able to get a good look at her. Her face was that of a woman in her late teens, with white-blonde hair she wore in a thick braid over her shoulder. Her eyes were a pale blue, her skin milk-white without freckle or flaw. She wore a sheer coral robe over a slinky pink nightgown, and I bet she was glad she couldn't feel the cold, because I was getting goosebumps just looking at her.

"Nice to meet you, Your Majesty," I said, skipping the niceties. "My name is Kat Palon, and we're here to help you stretch your muscles and enjoy some revenge."

Her cold expression didn't change. "Adrian's friend."

"The one and only. Since we have until sunset to get to know each other, I suggest we take a quick walk-around to make sure we don't have any more friends hiding in the shadows, and then we can sit down and chat about what the hell is going on."

13

Katerina

THE DRIVE BACK to the nest a few hours later was quiet but charged.

The skirmish with Harvey and the vampires had gotten my blood pumping, and based on the energy radiating off Orry, she was no less eager to get her fangs wet.

Emrick had left us, taking the faster way home to give Adrian and Barrett a heads up that we were coming. I hoped to be only a few minutes behind him.

It was just past seven o'clock in the evening, and the snowstorm was in full gale. I could barely see out my windshield, and keeping the car on the road was proving to be more of a challenge than taking down two vampires.

As I pulled onto the nest's street, Emrick appeared in my

rear-view mirror.

"Just thought I'd let you know, the party started without you."

I glanced at Orry, but the queen didn't react beyond clenching her teeth as she stared out the window.

"Oh?" I asked.

"Trillium discovered the imprisoned thralls missing and overheard a couple of vampires talking about how they'd lost contact with someone outside the nest. The fighting's started, but a bunch of vampires are down for the count. Looks like they were dosed with the same thing you were, Your Majesty."

"An attack they'll regret," Orry hissed.

I pressed on the gas, braving the black ice to reach the house a few minutes faster. Rhys was inside. If a vampire battle was on the menu, I didn't want him without defences.

I also didn't want to miss Orillia kicking some vampire ass.

Less than two minutes later, I pulled into the driveway, and Orry was out of the car before I turned off the engine. Emrick opened my door and kept close behind me as I followed the queen up the steps and into the house.

The bright lights and blast of heat hugged me after my few seconds outside, and I wished again I could have come here for peaceful reasons. Sitting in that hotel room with a cup of tea to watch the storm sounded blissful.

But watching some rebel vampires get their heads torn off

would be satisfying in a different way.

By the time we walked in, silence had fallen over the two dozen vampires spread across the foyer. No thralls were visible, but I suspected they were in the house somewhere. The air hummed with anticipation, a breath before battle.

"Your Majesty!" Rose rushed towards the queen and knelt at her feet. "I'm so glad you're all right. You had us worried. We—"

In less than a heartbeat, Orillia had the younger vampire's jaw gripped in her hand, her nails digging into the girl's flesh so deeply that thick black blood beaded around the tips.

"None of that, Rose," she said, her voice little more than a growl. "You're not going to have another lover take the fall for you this time."

Rose's eyes widened with feigned confusion, then she dropped the act and bared her teeth. She whipped out of Orry's hold and landed in a fighting stance, her meek demeanour nowhere to be found.

"I'm not hiding behind anyone anymore. On the contrary, I'm taking control. You've held us back for centuries, Orillia. Every time someone comes to you with a new idea, you knock it aside without deliberation. We've had enough."

Orillia laughed. "Your little group has been advocating for anarchy. Feeding without restriction, raising the number of thralls past the point of necessity. You're a glutton, Rose. Your way would tip the balance in this city and have the vampire hunters on our asses before the end of the month. You seek power you could never handle. I'm tempted to stand aside and let you try just to revel in how quickly you fail, but I won't abandon my nest to your childishness."

Rose screeched and threw herself at the queen. Orillia returned the attack with just as much fervour, though I noticed the wobble in her step and the tremor in her hand. She wasn't at full strength, and I worried she wouldn't be able to fight her way to victory on her own.

Fortunately, she wouldn't have to.

At Orry's cry, Trillium jumped into the fray, leading the rest of the vampires loyal to the queen, few as they were with the rest incapacitated.

Rose's people poured out of the kitchen and down the stairs, at least double the number of those fighting for Orillia.

How long had Rose been planning this coup? From what the queen suggested, the revolt last year had been her idea as well. Months of simpering and smirking, biding her time. Not so long for an immortal, but longer than I'd have been able to stomach.

"Kat, look out!"

The panic in Rhys's voice alerted me to the figure coming up on my left as the thralls spilled in after the vampires. I glanced up the stairs to find Rhys standing in the doorway of his room, the door cracked open an inch so he could peer down.

An inch too much.

"Get inside and close the door!" I shouted. Then all my attention was on the thralls. A dozen, two dozen, and none of them appearing to fight for the queen.

Somehow Rose had claimed them all and, by the surprise on Trillium's face, had already taken the initiative of increasing their numbers.

I hated taking human lives. As much as possible, I strove to avoid it. But when it came down to them or me—them or Rhys—my choice was simple.

Straining against the pull of my exhausted magic, I filled my hands with ice spikes and launched them at the people surrounding me, conscious of the vampires beyond them.

I didn't know how we would fight our way out of this. Emrick was weaving his way through the vampires, but he couldn't move fast enough, having to be careful not to lay hands on the wrong people. As the battle grew fevered, he had no choice but to give up.

He reappeared behind me, his back to mine, and I scowled as the thralls closed in. "Remember your promise, Emrick. Keep your hands to yourself."

"The gloves are on, Kat," he said over his shoulder.

I didn't know if a punch counted the same in Death's eyes as stealing a soul ahead of schedule, but short of forcing him out the door—difficult to do when the guy had eighty pounds of muscle on me—I would have to settle for that being good enough. At the very least, he could give me a shout if any of them got too close.

Soon, however, *close* wasn't the problem. Breathing was the problem.

The thralls seemed to have targeted me as a weak point, and I was crushed in the middle of the horde.

"You have to go," I called to Emrick as I dodged another blow.

He growled a curse and turned to me. "Whatever it takes, Kat. Promise me. Whatever it takes to get out of here."

"Go!"

Then he was gone, and I did my best to stab my ice spikes in the increasingly cramped space.

I hated to admit it, but I wished Barrett were with me. For all his faults, he knew how to work a crowd.

Screams and the reek of blood filled the air, and between arms, legs, and determined faces, I glimpsed the vampire ash piling up on the black floor. I had no idea who was winning, but the fact the thralls were fighting told me Rose was still undead. That any of us were fighting suggested Orillia was still kicking, too, otherwise I would be hearing less screaming, more crowing. But I wasn't about to hinge my approach on false confidence.

A fist lodged in my solar plexus, knocking the breath out of me, and a knife swiped across my chest. Burning pain followed the blow, so intense it made my head swim. With a curse, I forced more ice into my hands. My magic circled in my core, fighting me. I breathed through the pulsing discomfort as my fingers went numb, and the spikes slid from my grip.

With a grunt of frustration, pushed to last resorts, I drew on my heat and summoned my fire. The gloves contained the magic, and with full control, I pushed the flames outwards, lighting up the nearest thralls.

They panicked and tried to run, but the mob had pressed in too tightly. There was nowhere for them to go.

Only when the first bodies fell, consumed by the spreading fire, did I realize the danger I'd put myself in. I was crushed between them, no more able to escape the heat than they were. Smoke and the odor of charred flesh filled my nose, and I shoved against the burning bodies closest to me. My fingers shrieked at the pain of nerve endings burning, of skin cooking, peeling, melting, but desperation drove me, and finally I created enough space to drop to the floor in a crouch. Too many legs stood in my way, but at least down here, the smoke wasn't so thick, allowing me to hold on to consciousness while I figured out how to free myself from this mess.

The piercing lullaby of howling wolves cut through the agonized cries of burning human and tortured vampire, and relief cut through my fevered panic.

The thralls scattered, allowing me to push through the

fallen bodies to freedom, but the sight that greeted me turned my stomach.

A dozen wolves had arrived, and half of them were in the process of tearing the throats out of the rebel vampires. Rose and Orillia were locked fist to fist, their fangs bared. Rose was covered in blood, her clothes in tatters, and her expression one of frantic rage. Orillia's appearance was no tidier, but the only glint in her eye was one of cold retribution. She had no doubts that she would be victorious, and her confidence was terrifying.

I understood why Adrian enjoyed spending time with her.

Trillium and a few of the remaining loyal vampires battled around her, keeping the rebels off the queen so Orry could focus on the woman who had attempted to rip away her crown for her own selfish gain.

The other half of the shifter pack had targeted the thralls, and while it seemed as though their directive was to maim instead of kill, the carnage was no less horrific. Limbs lay scattered across the marble tile, and blood sprayed over the walls, turning the white columns with their nightshade blossoms a gruesome, mottled hue.

Barrett and Adrian fought among the shifters.

Adrian moved with his usual speed and grace, weaving his way through thrall and vampire without hesitation, his blades flying so quickly I saw nothing more than a glint in the light.

Barrett fought stiffly, concentrating on one target at a time and trusting Adrian to keep everyone else off him, but he was no less methodical or lethal for being injured.

The wound on my chest closed, and the blisters on my fingers faded, far from fully healed but the pain dulled enough to ignore. Exhilarated by the arrival of our reinforcements, my energy flared, and I returned to the battle, summoning ice spikes to help Barrett and the shifters take down the rest of the thralls.

Minutes later—or it could have been hours—the house was silent except for the panting breaths of the non-vampiric survivors.

One of the wolves shifted into a very tall, very wide, very naked man whose skin glistened with sweat. He eyed the mess and locked eyes with Orillia. "I consider our revenge for our lost wolves claimed, but once you've dealt with your nest, we'll be meeting to discuss the terms of our alliance."

With that warning, he struck his fist against his chest, and a blood-spattered Orry bowed her head.

I prayed to every god that might exist that I wouldn't be called in to mediate that conversation.

The wolves left as quickly as they'd come in, leaving only the vampires, me, and Barrett standing witness to the chaos that had ensued tonight in this beautiful home.

Rose and Orillia stood in the middle of the circle. Rose was the only rebel vampire standing, guarded on all sides by Orillia's people.

Trillium stood behind her, her fingers curled, her teeth bared. The others took their cue from her, standing at the ready in case their queen needed her but deferring to Orillia to make the final judgement.

"You've failed," the queen said. "For the last time."

Rose hissed. "It may not be me who defeats you, but your days are numbered. You can't live forever and expect things not to change."

Orillia flashed her fangs. "Oh, my dear, that's what you've never understood. You were looking to take things backwards, to the way they used to be. But that's not how immortality works. When you live in a world that changes this quickly, you have no choice but to move forward. Or die to prevent holding everyone else back."

So quickly I barely saw her move, she lashed out with her elongated talons and sliced across Rose's neck.

A gasp came from up the stairs—Rhys and I would be talking later about following instructions—but the vampires remained still, silent, not reacting at all as Rose's head slid from her shoulders and hit the floor with a squelch before the rest of her body followed.

14

Katerina

THE AFTERMATH OF the battle was quick—almost as if the vampires were used to cleaning up mass carnage.

I didn't want to think about that too closely, as it would mean popping in more often to see what they were up to, a task that was very low on my wish list. Somewhere under shovelling wyvern shit.

Barrett and Adrian found me standing by one of the columns. Barrett's wound had reopened, but he was standing on his own, so he'd be fine. Probably. Adrian's lips were dark and his cheeks were pink, suggesting he'd enjoyed himself on multiple levels during the fight. At least one of us had.

Emrick had never returned after I'd ordered him away. Not that I'd expected him to. Had been relieved he hadn't.

Happy, even.

I'd barely finished watching the last burns on my fingers fade when Orillia presented herself in four-inch crimson heels, cream-hued slacks, and a soft lilac blouse unbuttoned to her knock-out cleavage. Her white hair was pulled up in a loose French twist that would have taken me hours to imitate.

"Trillium made the right decision calling you," she said, as much to Adrian as to me.

Adrian bowed. "Your Majesty, I'm glad we could be of service. I would have regretted losing your companionship after the years we've enjoyed together."

Her gaze flicked to Barrett with a subtle smile, and I blinked, not wanting my thoughts to veer in any direction that even hinted at the subtext being alluded to here.

"I hope to see you all again shortly under more pleasant circumstances. Our Midsummer Masquerade, perhaps. For tonight, however, I have business to attend to with my nest."

Finding out how many traitors are left in the ranks.

That part went unsaid, but I read the room. Just as I read her silent dismissal.

A pat on the head, a "well done, thanks for saving my legacy," and off we went.

I hated dealing with vampires.

On the plus side, it meant we were free to go home, and I couldn't wait to get out of here, three shirts and one pair of leggings less.

Half an hour later, I stood next to my car. Rhys sat in the passenger seat, door closed, on the phone with Maera to give her the heads up that we would be on the road soon and home sometime in the small hours. I hoped he was censoring his story of what happened—or at least emphasizing the effort I'd made to keep him out of trouble—but I suspected I'd be in for a few narrowed looks and pointed comments about dragging her son into a vampire nest.

Maera was my housekeeper, caretaker, and companion, and I'd known her since she was born, but that never stopped her from going full *mom* on me.

Barrett sat behind the wheel of Adrian's car, grim-faced and staring straight ahead. He'd gone so far as to give me a nod before sliding gingerly into the seat, which I accepted as his version of an enthusiastic high-five.

We'd done the job well, quickly, and with no losses to the team. As far as Barrett was concerned, that was a win.

"Are you sure he should be driving?" I asked Adrian as I leaned my butt against my driver's side door. "He looks a bit... iffy."

Adrian shook his head, his dark eyes gleaming with affection. "He refused to let me take over. I suspect he would rather take the chance of blacking out behind the wheel than the more likely option of me driving us into a ditch."

I grinned. "I forgot. For all the modernities you've embraced, driving is not one of them. France is still reeling from that stint of yours through No Man's Land."

He barked a laugh. "Yes, but I gave the Germans something to gawk at, didn't I?" His mirth softened into nostalgia and soon shifted into something more knowing. "Watching you and Emrick work together today brought back many such memories."

I stiffened, my smile frozen in place. "Adrian."

He raised his hands. "I know. You two have your reasons. And I'm not saying they're not valid. But is staying apart truly the only option? You're both suffering for it, in more ways than one. I hate to see two of the people I care about most in the world in pain because of something that could be fixed."

"We've tried other ways. Many times."

Which he knew because he'd been there. He'd witnessed the arguments, been part of the brainstorming sessions on ways for Emrick to help me that didn't involve him sacrificing fragments of himself every time I wound up in danger. The result was me with weakened magic, Emrick breaking promises, and the three of us heartbroken and separated.

I pulled him in for a hug. "I'm sorry you're stuck in the

middle, my friend."

He squeezed me back tightly. "Be happy, cuore mio. It's all I ask. Life is too long to choose to be miserable."

With a kiss on my cheek, he pulled away and climbed into the SUV, raising his hand in farewell as Barrett drove off.

I slid into the driver's seat and slammed the door shut just as Rhys ended his call.

"You okay?" he asked, concern written in all the exhausted lines of his face.

"Peachy. Be grateful your past is still too short to catch up with you." I started the car and pulled into the road. "All right. Let's go home and face your mother."

Epilogue

Emrick

I WAITED A few days before checking in on Kat. She needed time to recover from her fun with the vampires, and I needed time to recover from Kat.

Maybe I should have stayed away longer, obeyed her order to leave her alone, but the pull between us was too strong to ignore.

Almost a thousand years, and I still didn't know whether that tug on our bond was a reflection of my desires or a response to hers. But I'd learned to listen to it even if more often than not the result was a renewal of Kat's fury with me.

Which I braced for tonight when her eyes narrowed on seeing me.

She sat in her Muskoka chair, phone on the table beside her, a cup of steaming tea in her hands. A dark grey terry-cloth robe hugged her bare shoulders, and a thick blanket was wrapped around her waist.

Anyone else might wonder what she was doing sitting outside on such a frigid night, but that was my Katerina. She'd told me the cold made her thoughts sharper. I suspected it had begun as a form of self-punishment, a discomfort she believed she deserved for failing her family, but that over the years had become a source of peace.

Without waiting to be invited, I dropped into the other chair. I hated these chairs. Before long, my legs would be asleep, my back would ache, and I'd struggle to get up, but I didn't comment, simply stared up at the stars through the barren branches.

Time ticked on, and the silence settled around us, as familiar as the scent of aloe and wisteria on her skin.

She broke it first. "Things can't go back to the way they were between us. I wish they could, but they can't."

My throat tightened. I hadn't expected her to say anything different, but it still hurt.

So many times I'd broken my promise to stay detached, to turn my back on her distress, but not once did I regret it. I feared what future awaited me if I gave up too much of myself, but if my choice was wasting away or losing her, I knew where I stood.

I also understood her position. If I became a wraith, she would be in the same situation I'd be in if she met her final death. Stuck for eternity with nothing but a gnawing, growing void in place of the love that had existed before.

But was what we had now any better?

"No going back," I agreed, and cleared my throat at the roughness lining my words. "What about finding a way forward?"

She sipped her tea and kept her gaze trained on the sky. But I caught the way her hands tightened around her mug and the glimmer of tears in her eyes before she blinked them away.

"I don't know," she said.

I relaxed in my chair in an attempt to get comfortable and tried to find solace in her answer. It wasn't a refusal.

We were immortal. Time had stopped for us, but that didn't mean we didn't change. While the possibility remained that we would find our way back to each other, I would cling to hope.

And I feared we would have plenty of opportunities to find out what lay ahead. Over the past few days, a sense of unease had woven through the afterlife and curled deep in my soul. Danger was coming, more of the past creeping up to threaten the future, and rumours hinted that Kat was at the heart of it.

My poor immortal sorceress who longed for peace and found enemies at every turn.

Whatever danger was coming, she wouldn't be alone. Whether she accepted it or not, my heart was hers. Side by side or back to back, I would stand with her, and we would face the future together.

Thank You for Reading

Thank you so much for taking a chance on an independent author. We're living in a wonderful age where it's easy to upload a book to the internet, but that doesn't reflect the blood, sweat, and tears that go into making a book the best version it can be. It takes time, patience, perseverance, and to have the final result end up in a new reader's hands is the best reward. You are the reason we keep writing, so thank you.

If you enjoyed the read, please help support the author by leaving a review at the retailer where you purchased the book. Reviews make a world of difference for an author, helping us reach new audiences and bringing more people into the worlds you've spent time in.

For exclusive character content, announcements, promotions, and special offers, sign up for Krista's mailing list at https://www.kristawalshauthor.com/pages/about-the-author

Acknowledgements

Kat & Emrick have been living in my head for so long, I'd begun to worry they'd never make it onto the page.

Three different versions of their story exist (completed drafts!), but I have the following people to thank for helping me shape them between 2009 and their final publication debut in 2023.

Megan Connell. Kat & Emrick's greatest believer and cheerleader. Thank you for continuing to push me to tell their story.

Kate Sparkes, because no book is ever "complete" in my mind without your input on it.

The FAKAs, hands down the best writing group I've ever been a part of. You helped me craft a story that is sure to find its people and have held my hand in giving these two immortals their best shot at success. I'm so grateful to every one of you.

Christopher Barnes, thank you for your eye and catching all my too-long and too-short sentences so they could be just right.

My ARC readers and street team, thank you for helping me make Kat's launch so much stronger than I could have on my own.

My Patrons! You've been with me every week, enjoying the teasers, encouraging me and motivating me to get it done. You guys are amazing!

My wonderful husband, Chris Reddie, and my beautiful daughter, you are my anchors in the maelstrom. Love to the moon and back.

And to my readers, I hope you fall in love with Kat & Emrick. I hope Kat's story over the next few books has you laughing and crying and awaiting the next adventure.

I can't wait to experience it with you.

About the Author

Known for witty, vivid characters, Krista Walsh never has more fun than getting them into trouble and taking her time getting them out.

When not writing, she can be found reading, gaming, or watching a film – anything to get lost in a good story.

She currently lives in Ottawa, Ontario with her husband, toddler, and epileptic blue heeler.

You can find her at www.kristawalshauthor.com or at the local Second Cup coffee shop... but only if you come bearing a Vanilla Bean Latte, half-sweet.

Other Works by Krista Walsh

Epic Fantasy

The Meratis Trilogy

The Cadis Trilogy

The Nayis Trilogy

Urban Fantasy

The Dark Descendants

The Ghostmaker Trilogy